D0536753

Franklin Wants a Badge

From an episode of the animated TV series *Franklin*
produced by Nelvana Limited, Neurones France s.a.r.l.
and Neurones Luxembourg S.A.

Based on the *Franklin* books by Paulette Bourgeois and
Brenda Clark.

TV tie-in adaptation written by Sharon Jennings
and illustrated by Shelley Southern, Jelena Sisic,
and Alice Sinkner.

Based on the TV episode *Franklin's Badge*,
written by Karen Moonah.

ISBN 0-439-43122-0

12 11 10 9 8 7 6 5 4 3 2 1   3 4 5 6 7/0

Printed in the U.S.A.   23
First Scholastic printing, October 2003

Kids Can Press is a *corus*™ Entertainment company

Franklin Wants a Badge

SCHOLASTIC INC.

New York   Toronto   London   Auckland   Sydney
Mexico City   New Delhi   Hong Kong   Buenos Aires

FRANKLIN belonged to the choir at school and the chess club at the library. He was on the soccer team at the park and the swim team at the pond. Tonight, Franklin was joining the Woodland Trailblazers. He could hardly wait to start earning badges.

Franklin hurried home after school. He rushed to his room and got out his brand-new Trailblazer uniform. He put on his vest and his hat. Then he fastened his belt and tied his scarf.

"I'm ready to go!" he declared.

His mother laughed.

"Trailblazers doesn't start for two more hours," she said. "You have time to do homework."

Franklin sighed.

At six o'clock, Franklin was waiting at the door.

"We've got to go," he called to his father. "I don't
want to be late for Trailblazers."

Franklin and his father headed to the town hall.
It was starting to get dark, and Franklin felt all shivery
with excitement. He ran ahead a little bit and called
back to his father.

"Come on," he urged. "I want to be the first one
to earn a badge!"

At the hall, Franklin left his father and went to the meeting room.

"Come join our circle," invited Leader Fox.

Franklin sat between Bear and Jack Rabbit. He stared at Jack Rabbit's vest.

"You sure have a lot of badges," he said.

"I've been a Trailblazer for three years," explained Jack Rabbit.

"Three years!" exclaimed Franklin. "I don't want to take *that* long to get my badges."

Soon the meeting got started. Franklin learned the Trailblazer promise.

"I will work hard, help others, and be cheerful," he recited.

He learned the Trailblazer call.
"A-WOOO! A-WOOO! A-WOOO!" howled Franklin.

He learned the Trailblazer handshake.

Franklin shook hands all around the circle.

He stopped at Leader Fox. "When do we get badges?" he asked.

Leader Fox smiled.

"Over the year, we'll be working on lots of badges," he replied. "There's a swimming badge and a skating badge and . . ."

Franklin interrupted.

"I can swim and skate," he said. "Can I get those badges now?"

"We'll earn those badges together," said Leader Fox. "We'll go skating in January and have a swimming party next June."

Franklin counted out the months on his fingers. January and June were far away.

Leader Fox called everyone over to the craft table.

"Right now, we're going to make kites," Leader Fox said. "Then we'll donate them to Woodland's Day Care Center."

"Next week, we'll get started on our Halloween costumes," he added. "We're going to put on a parade for the Children's Hospital."

"By November, you'll all have earned your Community Badge," he finished.

Everyone cheered, but Franklin frowned. November seemed almost as far away as January.

Leader Fox gave out fabric and ribbons and string.
Then he handed out glue and scissors and markers.
Soon everyone was busy making a kite.

And soon, there was a big mess on the floor.

"Who would like to volunteer for cleanup?" asked Leader Fox.

"Is it for a badge?" asked Franklin.

"It can be," Leader Fox replied. "If you clean up after craft time for the rest of the year, you will earn your Helper Badge."

"The rest of the year!" exclaimed Franklin. "No wonder it took three years for Jack Rabbit to get all those badges."

Franklin sighed as he swept up the garbage. He sighed even louder as he cleaned up the glue.

"Well done, Franklin," said Leader Fox. "You are demonstrating the Trailblazer promise — working hard and helping others."

"I thought he was supposed to be cheerful, too," pointed out Beaver.

Everyone laughed. Franklin managed a very tiny smile.

Franklin finished the cleanup and joined the others. He was just in time for snacks. He watched as Leader Fox put out glasses of milk and lots of chocolate chip cookies.

"Do we get snack time every week?" asked Franklin.

"Sure do," said Leader Fox. "Trailblazers work hard and need energy."

"Hmmm," said Franklin.

Then it was time for games. Leader Fox showed everyone how to play Find the Trail. Afterward, they played Climb the Mountain.

"Do we play games every week?" asked Franklin.

Leader Fox nodded.

"And now we're going to sing songs," he said. "Trailblazers get to have lots of fun."

"Hmmm," said Franklin.

Leader Fox called everyone back to the circle.
He held a carved walking stick in his hand.

"This is our Trailblazer staff," he said. "Every
week, the hardest-working Trailblazer gets to take
it home."

Leader Fox gave the staff to Franklin.
"Congratulations," he said. "You are a wonderful Trailblazer."
This time, Franklin's smile was huge.

Soon the meeting was over, and the Trailblazers hurried to find their parents. Franklin marched home with the Trailblazer walking stick. He told his father everything he had done and learned. He even demonstrated the Trailblazer call.

"A-WOOO! A-WOOO! A-WOOO!" cried Franklin into the dark.

"A-WOOO! A-WOOO! A-WOOO!" he heard back again and again.

"And you know the very best thing about Trailblazers?" Franklin said to his father.

"It will take me three whole years to earn all my badges!"